We are helping.

This is Bill, Hinda and me.

We are selling tickets.

This is me. I can jump.

This is Anna.

She paints well.

This is Ben.

He is a good cook.

This is Meg.

She is good at kicking.

This is Seth.

He is a good goalkeeper...

...but Meg is a

winner!